Dear Parent:
Your child's love of reading starts here!

Every child learns to read in a different way and at his or her own speed. You can help your young reader improve and become more confident by encouraging his or her own interests and abilities. You can also guide your child's spiritual development by reading stories with biblical values and Bible stories, like I Can Read! books published by Zonderkidz. From books your child reads with you to the first books he or she reads alone, there are I Can Read! books for every stage of reading:

SHARED READING
Basic language, word repetition, and whimsical illustrations, ideal for sharing with your emergent reader.

BEGINNING READING
Short sentences, familiar words, and simple concepts for children eager to read on their own.

READING WITH HELP
Engaging stories, longer sentences, and language play for developing readers.

READING ALONE
Complex plots, challenging vocabulary, and high-interest topics for the independent reader.

ADVANCED READING
Short paragraphs, chapters, and exciting themes for the perfect bridge to chapter books.

I Can Read! books have introduced children to the joy of reading since 1957. Featuring award-winning authors and illustrators and a fabulous cast of beloved characters, I Can Read! books set the standard for beginning readers.

A lifetime of discovery begins with the magical words **"I Can Read!"**

Visit www.icanread.com for information on enriching your child's reading experience.
Visit www.zonderkidz.com for more Zonderkidz I Can Read! titles.

Be kind and compassionate to one another,
forgiving each other, just as in Christ God forgave you.
—Ephesians 4:32

ZONDERKIDZ

Bob and Larry in the Case of the Missing Patience
Copyright © 2011 Big Idea Entertainment, LLC. VEGGIETALES®, character
names, likenesses and other indicia are trademarks of and copyrighted by Big Idea
Entertainment, LLC. All rights reserved.
Illustrations © 2011 by Big Idea Entertainment, Inc.

Requests for information should be addressed to:
Zonderkidz, 3900 Sparks Drive SE, Grand Rapids, Michigan 49546

ISBN 978-0-310-72730-9

All Scripture quotations, unless otherwise indicated, are taken from the Holy Bible,
New International Version®, NIV®. Copyright © 1973, 1978, 1984, 2011 by Biblica, Inc.™
Used by permission. All rights reserved worldwide.

Any Internet addresses (websites, blogs, etc.) and telephone numbers in this book
are offered as a resource. They are not intended in any way to be or imply an
endorsement by Zondervan, nor does Zondervan vouch for the content of these
sites and numbers for the life of this book.

Editor: Mary Hassinger
Art direction: Karen Poth
Cover design: Karen Poth
Interior design: Ron Eddy

Printed in China

17 18 19 20 • 21 20 19 18 17 16 15 14 13 12 11 10 9

I Can Read!

Bob and Larry in The Case of the Missing Patience

story by Karen Poth

Welcome to the City Detective Agency.

This is Bob and Larry.

They are GREAT detectives.

Bob carries his badge.

Larry carries his stuffed badger.

The badger helps Larry be brave.

One day, Bob and
Larry were teaching
a SWAT class.
Chief Nezzer came in.
He brought three new
detectives.

"This is the Pod Squad," Nezzer said.

"Teach them to be great detectives."

Bob and Larry were glad to help.

RING!

Bob picked up the phone.

Mrs. Carrot had seen the

Masked Door Slammer!

Bob and Larry had been looking

for the Door Slammer for weeks!

They had to hurry.
"Come on," Bob said
to the Pod Squad.
But they did not all
fit in Bob's car.

They took the Pod Squad's van.

Oh no! About halfway there,

the van stopped working.

The detectives were stuck!

Bob and Larry pushed the van.

The peas sang songs.

By the time they got to the scene of the
crime, the Door Slammer was gone.
"Sorry, fellas," said Mrs. Carrot.

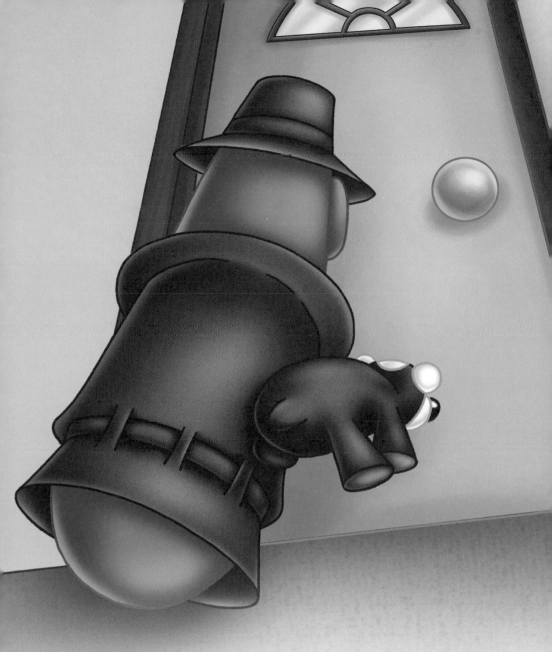

She closed the door.

"Rats!" said Larry.

"Looks like we missed him again!"

"This is your fault," Bob said
to the Pod Squad.

"Yeah," said Larry, "and now
we have to walk home!"

Bob and Larry hurt the

Pod Squad's feelings.

On their way back
through the park,
the detectives came
upon another crime!

"It was a bicycle!"

Madame Blueberry said.

"It knocked over my

hot dog cart and kept going!"

WET CEMENT

A trail of mustard led

Detectives Bob and Larry

to another crime!

The bicycle had ruined

Pa Grape's wet cement too!

This Bicycle Bandit had to be stopped!

Bob turned to the Pod Squad.

But the peas had fallen down a hill.

They were covered in yellow

police tape.

"Can't you do anything right?"

Bob asked.

The detectives followed the
bandit's trail.
It ended in Scooter's backyard.
They found the Bicycle Bandit!

It was Lil' Pea!

"Why did you do it?" Bob asked.

"Hold on," the Pod Squad said.

"We don't think this little fella

is a criminal."

Just then Laura Carrot ran

into the yard.

"It's all my fault!" Laura shouted.

"I was teaching Lil' Pea

how to ride his bike.

"He did everything wrong.

I said mean things and I pushed him!

I'm sorry, Lil' Pea. I wasn't very nice."

Then Bob realized something.
He and Larry had done the same
thing to the Pod Squad.

He and Larry were supposed to
teach the Pod Squad.
Instead they got angry with them.

"We're sorry," Bob said to the Pod Squad.

"Yeah, God wants us to use nice words

and encourage one another," Larry said.

Bob and Larry spent the
rest of the day teaching
the Pod Squad to be great detectives!

A person's wisdom yields patience; it is to one's glory to overlook an offense.

—Proverbs 19:11